The Frost Festival

by Melody Mews   illustrated by Ellen Stubbings

LITTLE SIMON

New York London Toronto Sydney New Delhi

LITTLE SIMON

An imprint of Simon & Schuster Children's Publishing Division

1230 Avenue of the Americas, New York, New York 10020

First Little Simon paperback edition September 2022. Copyright © 2022 by Simon & Schuster, Inc. All rights reserved, including the right of reproduction in whole or in part in any form. LITTLE SIMON is a registered trademark of Simon & Schuster, Inc., and associated colophon is a trademark of Simon & Schuster, Inc. For information about special discounts for bulk purchases, please contact Simon & Schuster Special Sales at 1-866-506-1949 or business@simonandschuster.com.

The Simon & Schuster Speakers Bureau can bring authors to your live event. For more information or to book an event contact the Simon & Schuster Speakers Bureau at 1-866-248-3049 or visit our website at www.simonspeakers.com.

Designed by Laura Roode. The text of this book was set in Banda.

Manufactured in the United States of America 0722 LAK 10 9 8 7 6 5 4 3 2 1

Library of Congress Cataloging-in-Publication Data

Names: Mews, Melody, author. | Stubbings, Ellen, illustrator. Title: The Frost Festival / by Melody Mews ; illustrated by Ellen Stubbings. Description: First Little Simon paperback edition. | New York : Little Simon, 2022. | Series: Itty Bitty Princess Kitty ; 11 | Audience: Ages 5–9 | Audience: Grades K–1 | Summary: Itty and her best friend, Luna Unicorn, enjoy all the snowy activities at the Frost Festival, but before Itty can judge the ice-sculpture competition, an ice pick goes missing and one sculptor blames another for stealing, so Itty must find the missing carving tool and find a way to settle the argument. Identifiers: LCCN 2021062022 (print) | LCCN 2021062023 (ebook) | ISBN 9781665912037 (paperback) | ISBN 9781665912044 (hardcover) | ISBN 9781665912051 (ebook) Subjects: CYAC: Ice carving—Fiction. | Festivals—Fiction. | Cats—Fiction. | Princesses—Fiction. | LCGFT: Novels. Classification: LCC PZ7.1.M4976 Fr 2022 (print) | LCC PZ7.1.M4976 (ebook) | DDC [Fic]—dc23

LC record available at https://lccn.loc.gov/2021062022

LC ebook record available at https://lccn.loc.gov/2021062023

Contents

A Special Invitation

Itty Bitty Princess Kitty looked around the royal garden and smiled. The flowers basked in the sunshine. They knew how lovely they looked. Itty had recently started caring for the garden, and because of her special attention, it had never looked better.

"See you soon," Itty called to the flowers as she headed toward the palace. She lived there with her parents, the King and Queen of Lollyland.

Itty walked into the grand entrance hall and heard her mom calling her from the throne room. Only very important announcements happened in the throne room! Itty hurried there.

"Hello, darling," Queen Kitty purred when Itty walked in. "You weren't running in the halls again, were you?"

Itty thought about how she had just raced there. She smiled sheepishly. "Sorry. I was just excited to hear the special announcement."

"I'd run for that too," King
Kitty said, winking at Itty.

"Anyway . . . ," the Queen said slowly, "we do have special news for you."

Itty's whiskers twitched with excitement.

"You've been invited to Frost Terra's Frost Festival!" said the Queen excitedly. "And that's not all. They've asked you to help judge the ice-sculpture competition. And it's all happening this weekend!"

Itty's eyes went wide. "That sounds amazing!" she cried. "I'll do it! I just have one question. . . ."

"What's that?" her father asked.

"Umm . . . what's a Frost Terra Frost Festival?"

Itty's parents burst out laughing. Then they explained that the festival happened once every five years in Frost Terra, and drew crowds from all over Lollyland.

"You were too young to remember, but here's a photo of you at the last one," the King said, holding out a photograph.

The picture showed Itty as a toddler. She was smiling in front of a grand ice sculpture that was shaped like a mermaid.

Itty definitely didn't remember that. But now she was old enough to make Frost Festival memories she'd never forget!

Better with a Friend

Itty knew there was one thing that could make the Frost Festival even better: her best friend, Luna Unicorn.

"Mom, can Luna come to the festival?"

"Sure." Queen Kitty smiled.

"Why don't you send a fairy to ask her parents' permission?"

"On it!" Itty cheered. Within moments, a palace messenger fairy, Sasha, was headed to Luna's house.

Itty went up to her bedroom to wait for Sasha's return.

"I hope they say yes," Itty said to herself as she paced.

"They did!"

Itty whirled around and saw Luna climbing off a cloud that had just arrived at Itty's bedroom window.

"I just had to tell you in person!" Luna shouted, glitter spraying from her horn.

Just then Sasha flew in Itty's window. She raised her tiny trumpet to her lips, ready to announce what Luna's parents had said. Then she spotted Luna and realized she'd already shared the news.

"Hmph!" Sasha stomped her feet.

"Oops. Sorry," Luna said to the fairy. She knew as well as Itty that fairies did not like their announcements to be interrupted.

"Thanks, Sasha!" Itty added as the frustrated fairy flew out the window.

"So tell me everything you
know about this Frost Festival,"
Luna said.

"I don't know much yet," Itty
admitted. "I was really little the
last time it happened. But my

parents have this photo album of pictures from that time. Want to look at it with me?"

Luna nodded enthusiastically, and the two friends sat down and opened the album.

There were photos of Lollyland animals in cozy sweaters and other winter gear, enjoying every winter sport imaginable, like sledding, skiing, and ice-skating.

And then there were the pictures of the yummy festival treats.

"That's a shaved-ice booth!" Luna exclaimed. "Oooh . . . and a hot-chocolate stand!"

Itty focused on the photos of the ice-sculpture contest. From all the animals gathered around the magnificent sculptures, one

thing seemed certain: In a festival filled with wonderful attractions, the ice-sculpture contest seemed to be the most exciting!

The Perfect Present

A few days later Luna was back at Itty's, trying to help her decide what to wear to the festival—which they were about to leave for. Luna was decked out in a bright blue ski suit with rainbow trim.

"What about this?" Itty modeled a pink sweater with a snowflake pattern.

"I like that," Luna said. "I just wish it were . . . fancier. Aren't judges supposed to look fancy?"

"Not necessarily!" The Queen swept into Itty's room, holding a silver box. "But this might be the perfect finishing touch."

The Queen smiled as she handed the box to Itty. "Your father and I asked the royal jeweler to create something special for you to wear today. We hope you like it."

Itty lifted the box lid and saw something sparkly nestled inside. "Is it . . . ," Itty began. Then she gasped. "A new tiara?"

That's exactly what it was. Itty had other tiaras, of course; each one had a special meaning. This one had glittering crystals that created a delicate snowflake pattern. When Itty put it on, it looked as if she had a ring of snowflakes dancing around her head.

"That is the prettiest, snowiest tiara I have ever seen!" Luna squealed.

"I love it," Itty said, giving her mom a hug. "Thank you so much!"

And then it was time to leave for Frost Terra. Itty and Luna settled onto the cloud that had arrived to take them. They waved goodbye to the King and Queen.

Then the cloud sped off. Itty and Luna were quiet for a while, admiring the landscape below. After a bit the air started to get colder, and Itty knew they must be getting close to Frost Terra.

Suddenly the cloud zoomed upward. Itty and Luna exchanged a confused look. Why was the cloud going higher instead of lower?

And then they saw it looming above . . . a majestic, snowy mountaintop. Frost Terra was at the tippy-top of Lollyland!

♥ chapter 4 ♥

Welcome to Frost Terra!

At the top of the mountain, the cloud coasted to a gentle stop. The first thing Itty noticed about Frost Terra was just how chilly it was. The second thing she noticed was the grand ice palace.

Made entirely of carved ice, the palace looked like something out of a fairy-tale book. There was even a moat—but the moat was an ice-skating rink!

"Hello, Princess! What do you think?"

Itty turned and saw a friendly looking brown bear who was wearing a glittery snowsuit.

"It's amazing," Itty replied.

The bear smiled wide. "We think so too! Welcome to Frost Terra, Princess Itty. I'm Barry Bear, the head organizer of this festival. We're delighted to have you here!"

"I'm delighted to be here," Itty responded politely. "This is my friend, Luna Unicorn."

As Luna said hello to Barry, Itty continued to admire the palace. "I can't believe how huge it is!"

Barry's chest puffed out proudly. "That's why we can only hold the festival every five years. It takes five years to complete each new ice palace. This year's palace is the biggest one ever." Barry paused. "Since you're a guest judge for

the ice-sculpture contest, we had
to make sure our palace was fit
for a princess."

"It definitely is," Itty assured
him.

"What time does the sculpture
contest begin?" Luna asked.

"In a few hours." Barry handed the girls a map. "This map includes all the events. Go walk around and enjoy yourselves. We'll see you later for the contest."

As Barry walked away, two bulldogs decked out in snow gear passed by.

"One of the Moose twins will probably win the sculpture contest this year," one bulldog said to the other.

"Marty or Mimi?" the other bulldog said. "Well, they do come from a family of sculptors. You're probably right."

"So!" Luna said, glitter spouting from her horn. "What should we do first?"

"I think . . . ," Itty began, her eyes drifting to the ice rink moat, "we should go ice-skating!"

Ice Is Nice

"I didn't know ice-skating was so hard!" Luna panted as she wobbled along the edge of the rink.

"I didn't know you'd never skated before." Itty giggled. "Should we do something else?"

Luna had a determined look on her face. "I want to do this! You go ahead and skate while I try to find my balance."

"Are you sure?" Itty asked.

"Positive!" Luna nodded.

Itty grinned and sped off. She waved to the other skaters, who were excited to see Lollyland's princess. She skated just a few rounds and then returned to Luna.

At the center of the rink, a flamingo in a flowy skirt was finishing up a routine. She twirled, jumped, and landed gracefully.

Itty and Luna applauded.

The flamingo skated over to

them. "Thanks for the applause! I'm Francie!"

Itty and Luna introduced themselves, and Luna explained that she had never skated before.

"Maybe Itty and I can help you," Francie suggested.

Francie was right. With two
friends to help, Luna managed to
let go of the railing and take a lap
around the rink. It was a wobbly
lap, but she did it!

Soon after, Itty and Luna said goodbye to Francie and decided to try another sport: sledding!

Itty loved the feeling of the wind whipping her fur. And Luna definitely had more fun with this winter activity.

After all that sledding and skating, the friends had worked up an appetite. They decided it was time to check out the festival's food stands.

"Everything looks delicious!" Luna exclaimed.

"Try the shaved ice," said a friendly looking penguin. "It's the best treat at the festival!"

"Plain shaved ice sounds kind of boring," Luna whispered as they checked out one of the shaved-ice booths, where a vendor was scooping ice out of a freezer.

"He adds flavored syrup." Itty giggled. "I think we should try it."

Then she noticed the sign that listed all the flavors. There was Razz-Ma-Tazz Raspberry and Bubblegum Chip and Very Vanilla Honey. She pointed out the sign to Luna and said, "But I don't know how we're ever going to choose a flavor!"

♥ chapter 6 ♥

Luna Takes Charge

Eventually, Itty decided to try the Sugarplum Strawberry. Luna went with Purple Mango.

Using a special scooper tool, the vendor rabbit scooped out freshly shaved ice and piled it into bowls. Then he poured syrup on both.

"Enjoy!" he said.

Itty tried a spoonful of her shaved ice. A smile spread over her face. It tasted like the juiciest strawberry in the world. It was frosty and delicious!

"We need a shaved-ice stand in Goodie Grove," Luna cheered after tasting hers.

The girls decided to walk around as they finished their treats. Close by was the tent where the sculptors were working on their ice creations.

The in-progress sculptures were very impressive. Itty noticed snowpeople, snowflakes, a frog, a penguin, a reindeer, and even an igloo.

Then Itty spotted the most ambitious sculpture she had seen so far: a tiny version of the festival's ice palace.

"I hope it's okay that I'm here," Itty whispered to Luna. It suddenly occurred to her that maybe she wasn't supposed to see the sculptures beforehand.

"I think it's more than okay," Luna assured her. "In fact, I think you should introduce yourself. I bet the contestants would love to meet you."

Itty liked Luna's idea, but she suddenly felt a little shy. What was she supposed to do, announce to everyone in the tent who she was?

But she didn't have to. At that moment, several sculptors rushed over.

♥ chapter 7 ♥

The Competition Heats Up

"Oh, it's so nice to meet you," said a monkey wearing a puffy coat.

"We're honored to have you here," added a smiling panda.

"We appreciate you coming all this way!" an alligator said, stepping forward.

Itty recognized her as the sculptor who'd been working on the ice palace. "We know Frost Terra is a bit of a long ride! I'm Ally, by the way. You must tell us if you need anything."

"I'm so happy to be here!" Itty said genuinely. "Actually, I'd love to learn more about ice sculpting. What's that special tool you're holding?"

But before Ally could answer, a commotion broke out at the other side of the tent.

Itty and the group walked over to see what was happening. It wasn't hard to find the source of the commotion: two moose were nose to nose, yelling at each other.

"You stole my ice pick!" one moose shouted.

"No, I didn't!" the other moose shouted back.

"Then you hid it, Mimi!" the first moose insisted. "You're trying to sabotage me!"

"Take that back, Marty!" the moose named Mimi responded angrily, her hooves on her hips.

Marty and Mimi Moose? Itty remembered hearing their names earlier—the two bulldogs had been talking about them and how they came from a family of ice sculptors.

Itty started to approach to see if she could help, but Marty stomped away. Mimi stomped away in the other direction.

"I guess ice sculpting gets pretty competitive," Luna whispered.

Itty looked around at all the other contestants, who seemed

to be getting along so well, and frowned. She hoped the twins would work things out before the competition!

♥ chapter 8 ♥

An Icy Mystery

Itty and Luna were about to leave when Ally Alligator said, "Do you still want to come check out my tools?"

Itty had to admit she felt a little uncomfortable still being in the tent. But Ally seemed nice, and Itty had said she wanted to see the tools. So she followed Ally to her workstation.

"I work with ice picks. I use different sizes for different techniques," Ally explained.

Ally's tools reminded Itty of the scooper the rabbit at the shaved-ice booth had used. Of course, the rabbit's tool had a scooped end instead of a sharp end, but the handles looked similar.

Ally showed Itty how she'd used the smallest tool to carve little details into the ice sculpture.

"Thank you for showing me!" said Itty. "I can't wait to look closer when I judge the competition. For now, I think Luna and I are going to check out the snow people and snow animals over there."

As Itty and Luna headed toward the exit, they noticed that Mimi and Marty were back together. And back to arguing.

Itty approached the two moose.
As they saw Itty, they
immediately stopped arguing.
They looked a little embarrassed.

"I'm sorry to interrupt. Is
everything okay?" Itty asked.

"No, *we're* sorry," Mimi said
with a sigh. "We didn't mean
to cause problems. But my twin
thinks I stole his favorite ice pick!"

"Do you think maybe it's just misplaced?" Itty asked. "What if Luna and I look for it?"

"That would be great," Marty said appreciatively. "If Mimi really didn't steal it—"

"I didn't!" Mimi cut in.

"Then it shouldn't be too hard to find," finished

Marty. "It's just like Mimi's, but mine has a blue handle."

Mimi held up her red-handled pick.

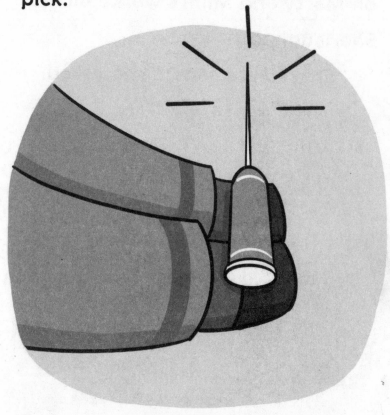

"We'll search the tent," Itty promised. Just then she noticed a whole bunch of shaved-ice bowls on Marty and Mimi's workbenches. She laughed.

"Shaved-ice fans?" she asked.

Mimi smiled. "It's the best part of the festival!" she said. "Well, that and the ice-sculpture competition." She explained that a vendor had come around earlier offering shaved ice to all the contestants. But she'd barely gotten to eat hers because that's when Marty's tool went missing and they started fighting.

Itty promised they'd look hard for the tool. She and Luna said goodbye and went off to search the tent. They looked over all the different workstations, under tables, and in the snow. But they could not find the ice pick anywhere.

"What next?" Luna sighed.

Itty gasped as she had a sudden thought. "Shaved ice!" she cried.

Case Closed

Luna frowned. "Is now really the time for more treats?" she asked. "We need to find the missing tool!" Itty grinned and pulled Luna out of the tent.

"I have an idea about what might have happened," Itty explained as she rushed toward the food pavilion. "Mimi said one of the vendors gave shaved ice to every contestant, but that she barely got to finish hers because it was right around that time that Marty's tool went missing."

Luna scratched her head. "I'm not sure I'm following. . . ."

"The ice picks look a lot like the ice scoopers. What if the vendor accidentally picked up Marty's tool, thinking it was a scooper?"

"Of course!" Luna yelled as they walked to the food stands. "Now we just need to figure out which vendor gave out the shaved ice."

"Oh, right." Itty looked around. There were dozens of shaved-ice vendors. How were they going to find the *one*?

"I know!" Luna squealed, glitter flying from her horn. "I just remembered—I saw the bowls on their benches

too. They were blue-striped bowls, and look—" Luna pointed across the pavilion. "That booth is using blue-striped bowls."

The friends rushed over to the shaved-ice stand and explained to the ferret working there what they were looking for.

"I don't think I have it, but let me double-check."

The ferret rummaged through the back of the stand. A moment later he popped up . . . holding the blue-handled ice pick!

"I'm so sorry! I don't know how
that happened!"

"It was an honest mistake,"
Luna said kindly.

The ferret smiled gratefully, and Itty and Luna rushed back to the tent to return the missing tool to Marty.

Itty just hoped there was enough time left for Marty to finish his sculpture!

And the
Winner Is . . .

"Princess Itty, do you have a minute?"

Itty smiled as the Moose twins approached her. "Marty, I saw that your sculpture made it into the competition. I'm glad you were able to finish!" Itty said.

"Well, it's all thanks to you for finding my tool," Marty replied.

"We also wanted to say thank you for helping us sort things out," said Mimi. "We realized we're probably too quick to blame each other."

"And we already agreed that no matter who wins, we won't fight about it," added Marty with a smile.

Itty was happy to hear this . . . because they were about to announce the winners!

Itty walked to the stage to join the rest of the judges.

Everyone had agreed that, as guest judge, Itty should declare the winner. She stepped forward to address the large crowd that had gathered.

"First, I just want to say that everyone did such a great job!" Itty began. "And now for the ribbons. Third-place ribbon goes to . . .

Marty Moose for his snowflake
sculpture!"

In the crowd Mimi gave her
brother a big hug.

"The   second-place   ribbon
goes to . . . Mimi Moose for her
lighthouse sculpture!"

"That's my twin!" Marty yelled
proudly.

"And first place goes to . . ." Itty paused dramatically. "Ally Alligator for her ice palace sculpture!"

Ally beamed, and Itty saw Marty and Mimi congratulating her.

Itty gave the winners their ribbons and everyone posed for pictures.

Just then, fireworks started bursting in the sky. Itty and Luna, and their new friends the Moose twins and Ally Alligator, posed for one more picture together. Between the blazing fireworks and the glimmering ice sculptures, Itty knew it was going to make for a fantastic photo.

And a memory she would never forget!

CLICK!

........cele..........

Here's a sneak peek at Itty's next royal adventure!

........ngcno.........

Itty Bitty Princess Kitty was sound asleep when something woke her up. She sat up in bed. It was still dark in her room. What had awakened her?

Itty was just about to snuggle back under the covers when she heard a sound. And not just any sound. It was the mermaids from Mermaid Cove singing! As Itty listened, the mermaids sang eight notes, which meant . . . she had overslept!

Itty sprang from bed. She had to get ready for school quickly! She couldn't believe she had slept so late. Her parents, the King and Queen of Lollyland, must have too, or surely one of them would have knocked on her door. Itty was grabbing her backpack when she heard the mermaids again. This time Itty heard *six* notes, which didn't make any sense. Itty peered out the window and saw that it was still dark outside. It wasn't usually dark when she left for school.

"Itty, slow down," Queen Kitty murmured sleepily as Itty sped through the royal foyer.

"But, Mom, I'm going to be late for school!"

"Late?" The Queen looked confused. "Darling, you don't have to leave for another hour. Why are you up so early?"

Now Itty was confused!